I Am Sofia

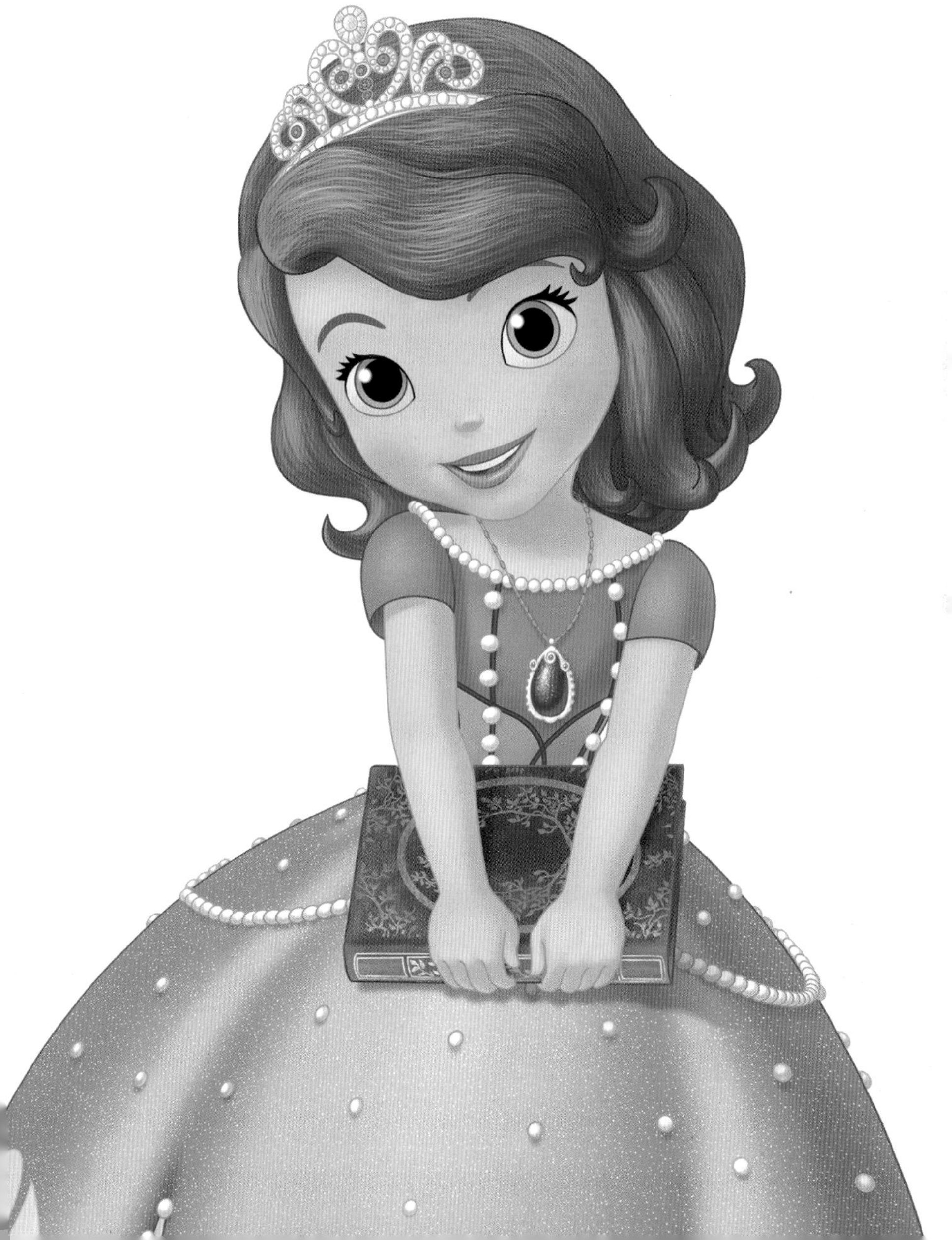

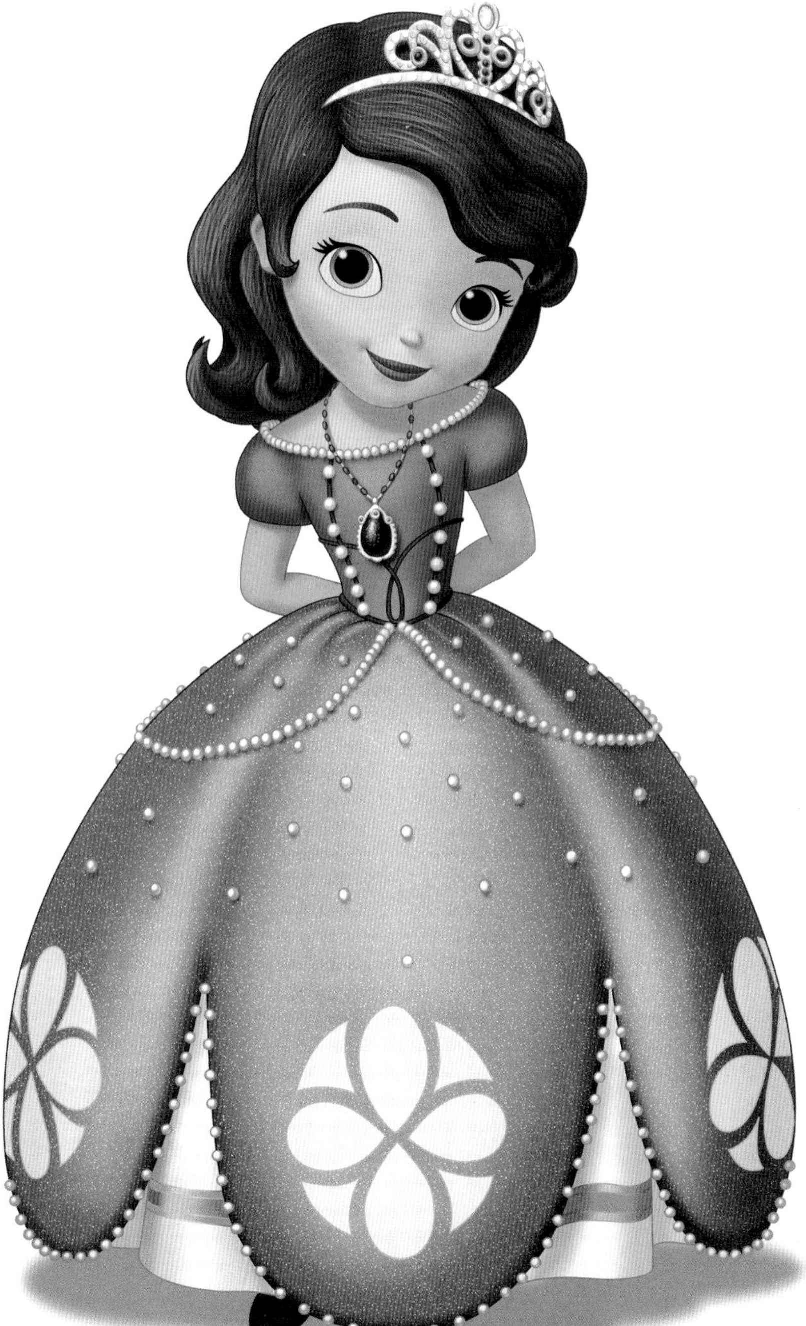

I am a daughter.

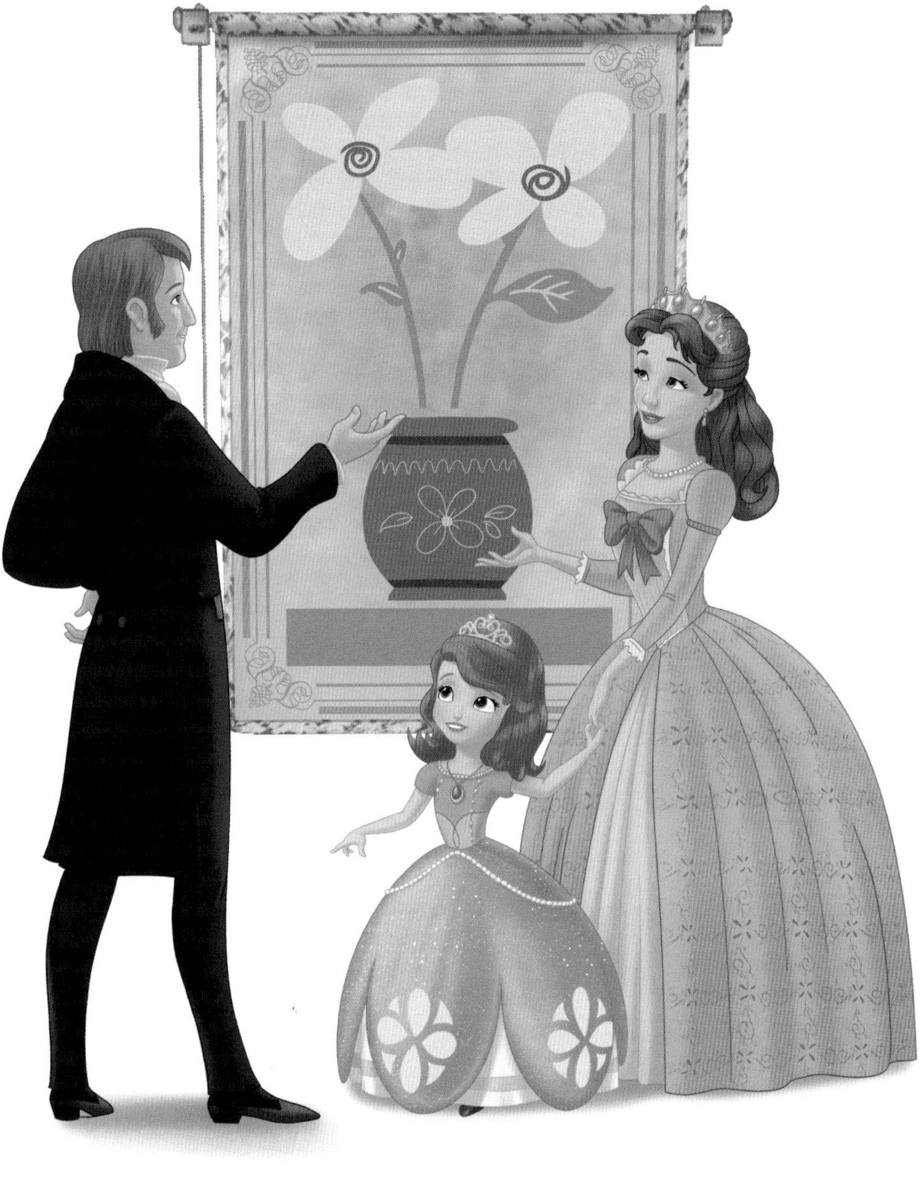

I am a sister.

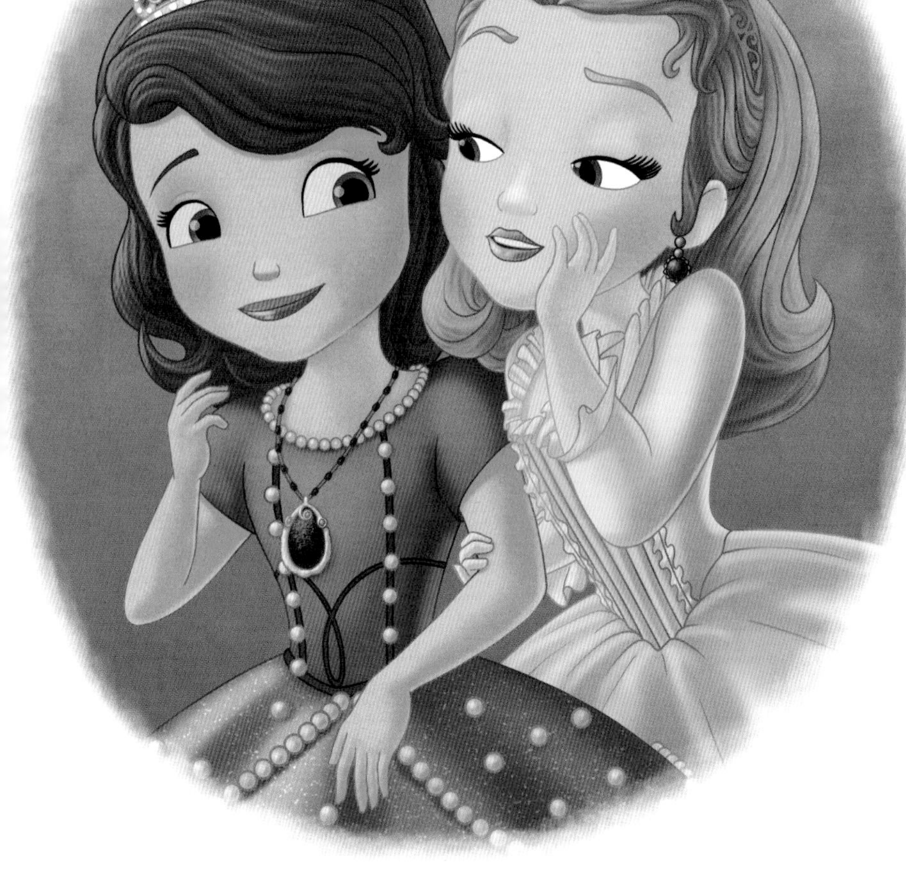

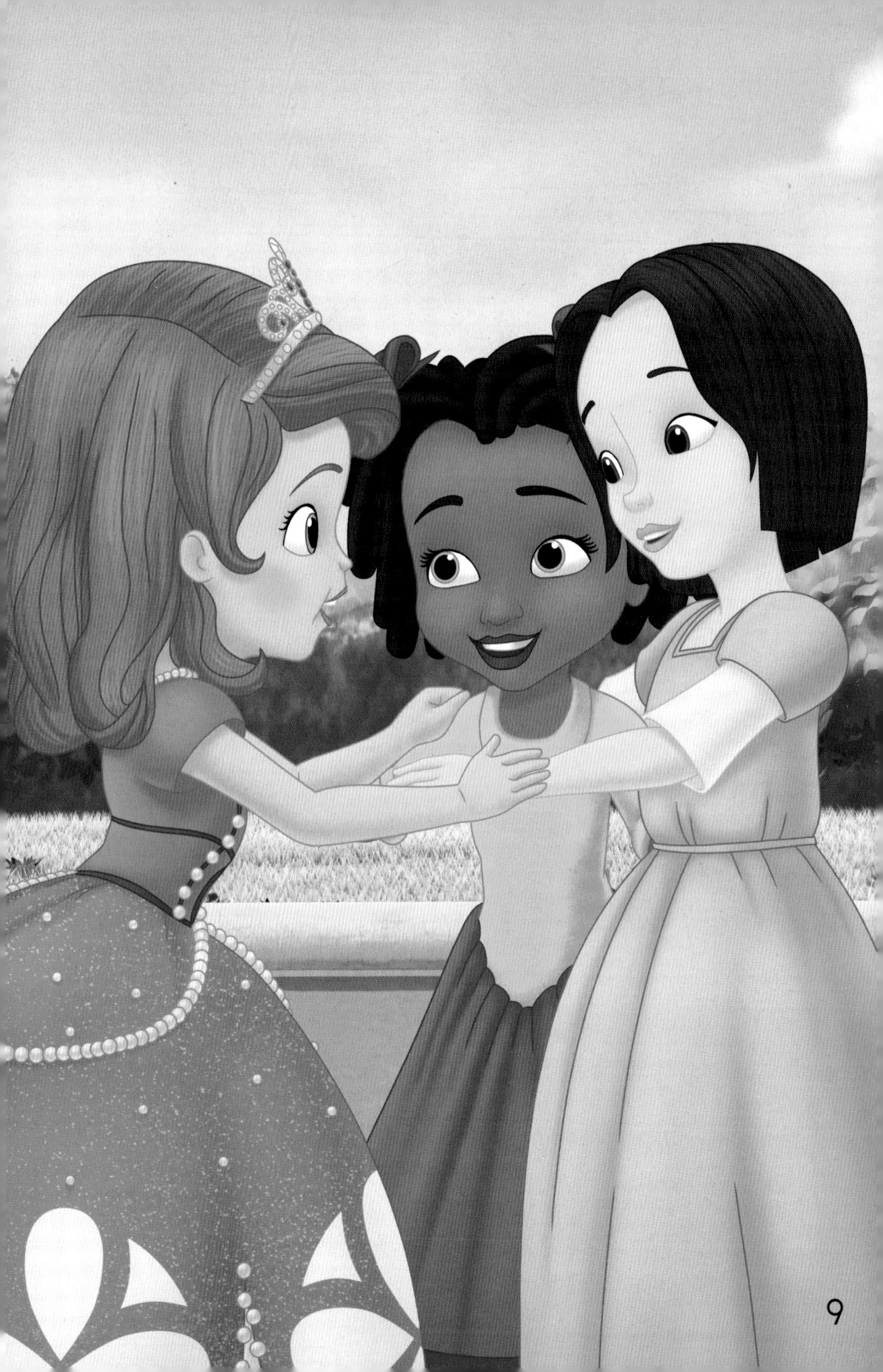

I am a student.

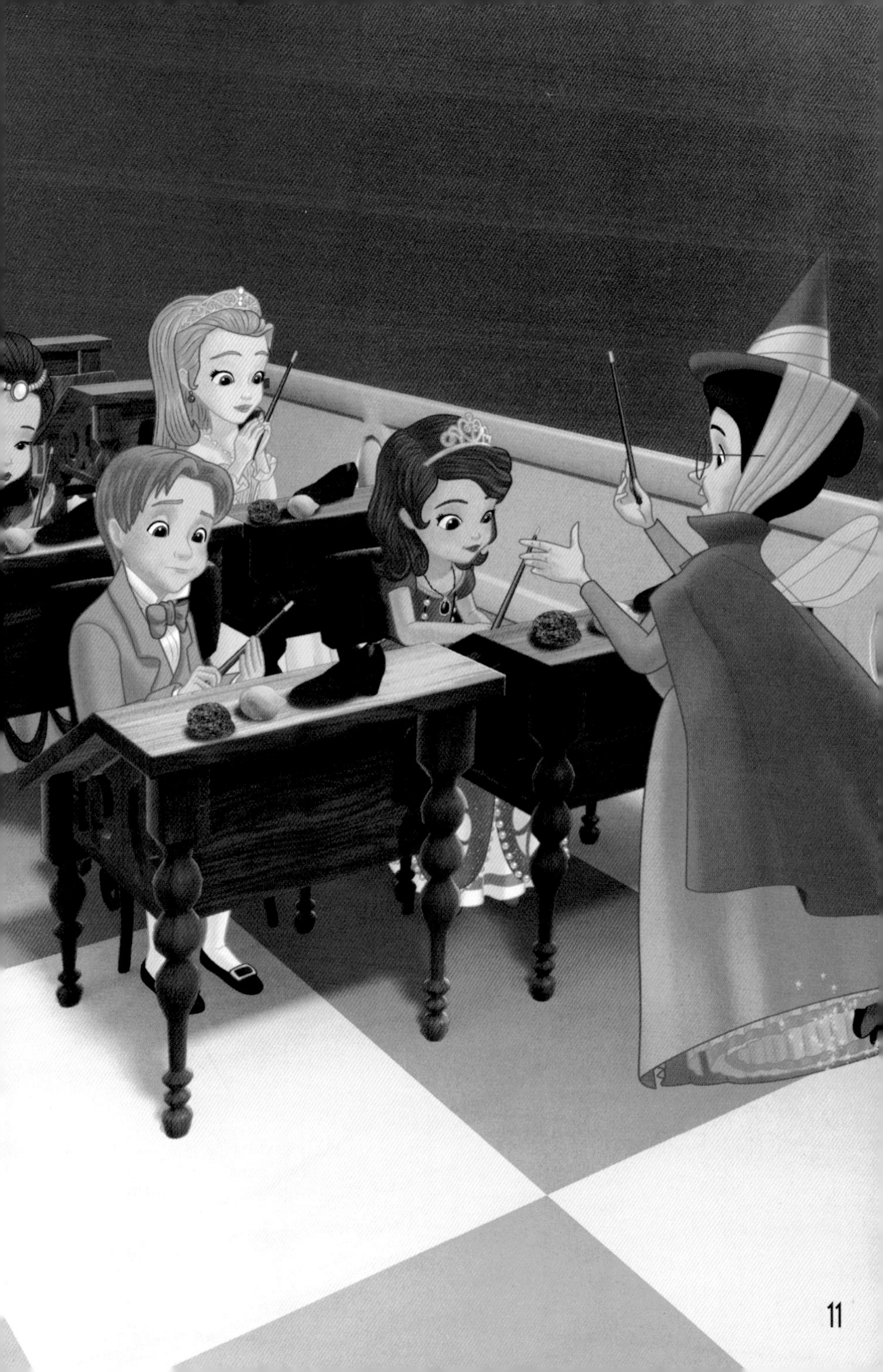

I am Sofia.

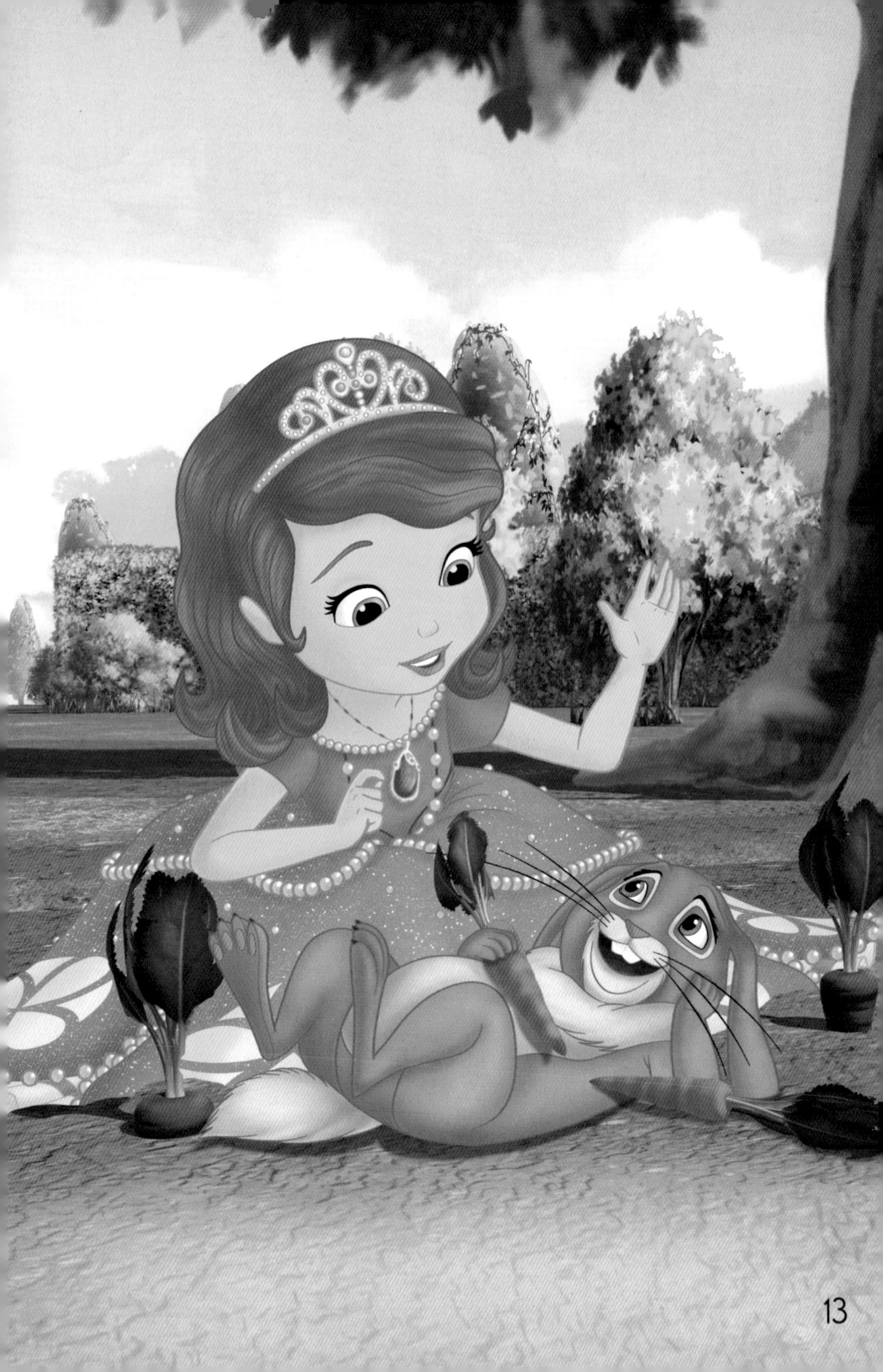

Who are you?

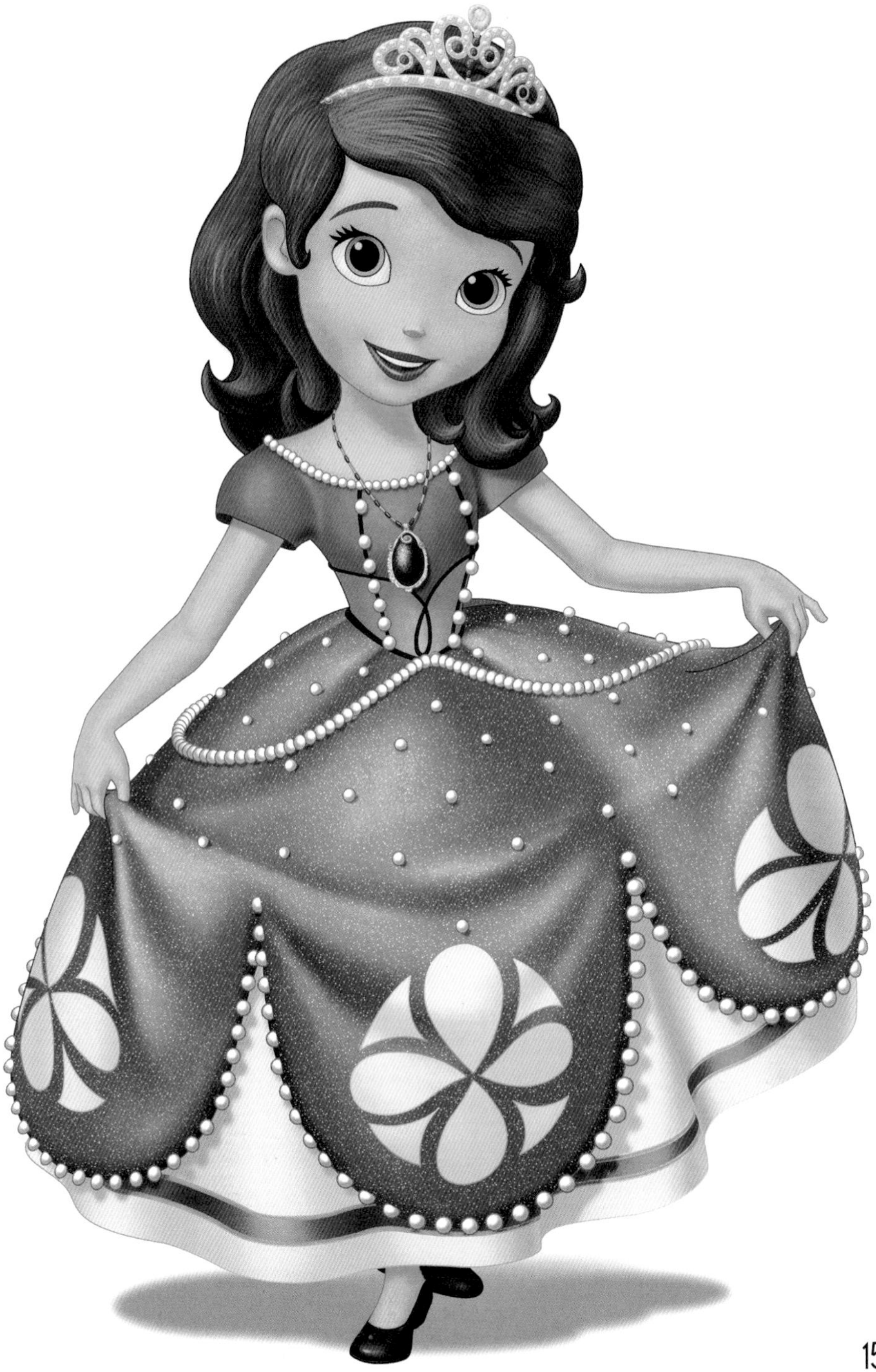

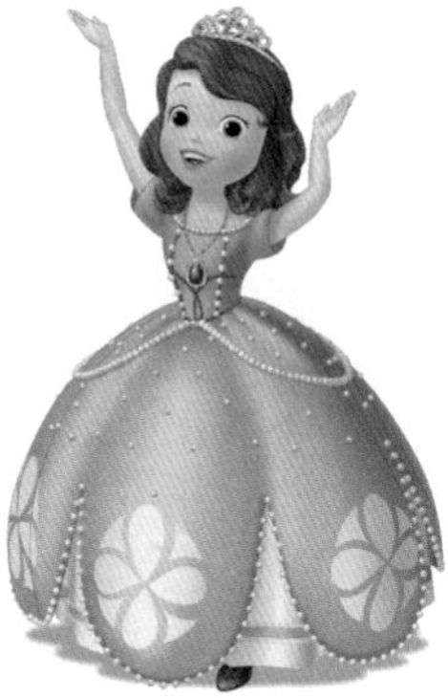